Spring Is Here, Hello Kitty!

by Kimberly Weinberger

illustrated by Sachiho Hino

SCHOLASTIC INC.

READER

© 1976, 2013 SANRIO CO., LTD. Used Under License.

All rights reserved. Published by Scholastic Inc., *Publishers since 1920.* SCHOLASTIC and associated logos
are trademarks and/or registered trademarks of Scholastic Inc.

The publisher does not have any control over and does not assume any responsibility for author or third-
party websites or their content.

No part of this publication may be reproduced, stored in a retrieval system, or transmitted in any form or
by any means, electronic, mechanical, photocopying, recording, or otherwise, without written permission
of the publisher. For information regarding permission, write to Scholastic Inc., Attention: Permissions
Department, 557 Broadway, New York, NY 10012.

This book is a work of fiction. Names, characters, places, and incidents are either the product of the
author's imagination or are used fictitiously, and any resemblance to actual persons, living or dead,
business establishments, events, or locales is entirely coincidental.

ISBN 978-1-338-11364-8

10 9 8 7 6 5 4 3 2 1   17 18 19 20 21

Printed in the U.S.A.   40

First printing 2017
Book design by Angela Jun

Spring is here!
Hello Kitty is very happy.
She and her friends plan to have
a picnic in the park.

Mama helped Hello Kitty pack
a picnic lunch.

Mama even baked an apple pie
for dessert!

Hello Kitty's friends arrived.
Jodie brought a blanket.

Tracy brought a ball.
And Fifi brought cups for juice.

Hello Kitty and her friends walked
to the park.

It was a beautiful day for a picnic.

Hello Kitty stopped at the entrance
to the park.

She couldn't believe her eyes.
There was garbage everywhere!

There was no place to have a picnic.

Hello Kitty and her friends wondered
what to do.

Hello Kitty sat down to think.

They all decided to clean up the park!

Hello Kitty and her friends hurried
back to Hello Kitty's house.

Mama was proud of their idea to clean
the park.

Mama brought out a stack of trash bags.

She found four pairs of gloves.

Mama gave everyone a snack first.
She brought out shiny red apples and
sliced cheese.

The snacks were delicious.
They would give everyone a lot of energy
to clean the park!

Hello Kitty and her friends finished their snack.

They each took a trash bag.
They each took a pair of gloves.

On the way back to the park,
Hello Kitty saw a robin in a tree.

The bird sang happily.

Hello Kitty, Jodie, Tracy, and Fifi
started right to work.

They picked up every piece of trash.
Soon the trash bags were filled.

Finally the park was clean.

It was time for their picnic.

Back at Hello Kitty's house,
Mama had the picnic basket ready.

The friends returned to the park together.

Picnics are fun. And so is spending time
with friends.
Happy spring!